ICE JOURNEY

Written by
GLEN DOWNEY

Illustrated by
GLENN BRUCKER

URSULA

BRUNO

MABEL

TUVAAQ

FICTIONAL CHARACTERS

URSULA: A giant short-faced bear. She must race to save her brother Bruno before it is too late.

BRUNO: Just a bear cub, Bruno is in a struggle for his life.

MABEL: A woolly mammoth who befriends Ursula.

TUVAAQ: A cave-dwelling hunter who has something in common with Ursula.

DON SMILO: A saber-toothed cat who kills Ursula's mother and goes after Bruno.

Contents

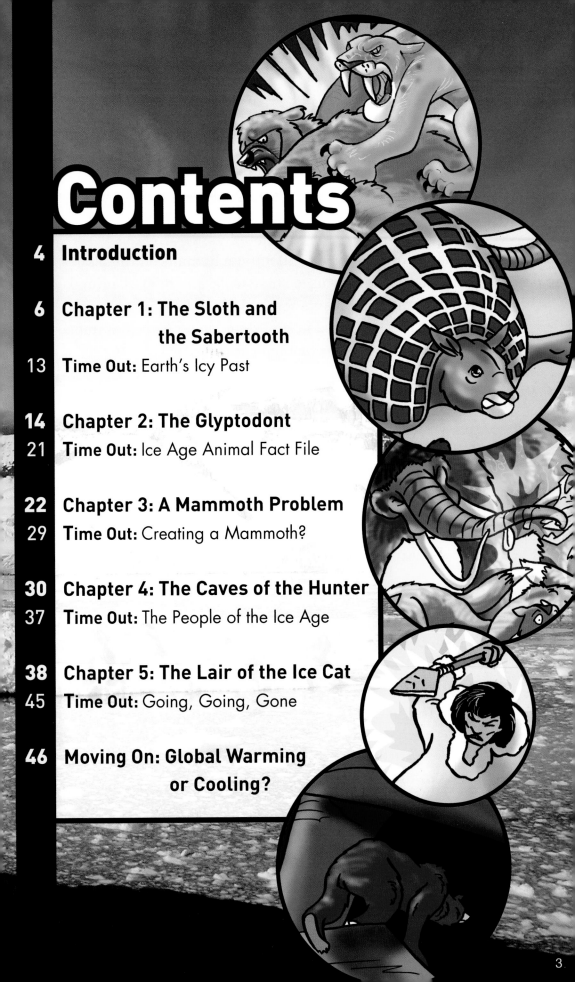

Fourteen thousand years ago, the climate was harsh and cold. Most of North America and Europe was covered with thick sheets of ice. Strange creatures roamed the snowy wastelands. Many seas were frozen, and the oceans were much lower than today. It was the Ice Age.

There were only five to 10 million humans on the planet at the time. They used stone tools, and hunted animals and gathered plants for food. They lived in caves and could be attacked at any time by dangerous animals such as the saber-toothed cat.

The letters B.C.E. stand for "Before Common Era." The years before the Common Era are counted backward, so the greater the number, the longer ago it was. For example, 30,000 B.C.E. is farther in the past than 20,000 B.C.E.

Two million years ago	30,000 B.C.E.	20,000 B.C.E.	15,000 B.C.E.
The most recent Ice Age begins.	A land bridge between Asia and North America is formed, allowing for the migration of plants, animals, and humans.	The Ice Age reaches its peak.	The earliest evidence of human settlement in North America.

Among the animals of the Ice Age was the giant short-faced bear. It was a meat-eating hunter and scavenger. It was even larger and heavier than the grizzly bear. It lived on the open plains of North America. As with the other animals of its time, life for the giant short-faced bear was a daily struggle …

WHAT'S THE STORY? This story is set in an actual time and place, but the characters and events in it are fictitious.

12,000 B.C.E. »	10,000 B.C.E. »	9,000 B.C.E. »	1,840 C.E. »
The global climate begins to warm up.	The giant short-faced bear becomes extinct.	The Ice Age comes to an end. Many animals become extinct.	Louis Agassiz, a Swiss scientist, is the first to argue that there was an Ice Age on Earth.

URSULA ARRIVES AT THE CAVE WHERE SHE LIVES WITH HER MOTHER AND BROTHER. SHE SENSES TROUBLE.

WAIT — SOMETHING'S WRONG ...

A SABER-TOOTHED CAT. IT'S DON SMILO! NO-O-O!

GRRR!

URSULA'S MOTHER IS BEING ATTACKED BY DON SMILO, THE SABER-TOOTHED CAT!

BRUNO, RUN!

MOTHER!!!

HMM ... I'D HOPED TO EAT MY KILL.

NEXT TIME, I'LL GO AFTER THE LITTLE ONE FIRST!

STARTLED, DON SMILO SLINKS AWAY.

URSULA HAS NO CHOICE BUT TO GO LOOKING FOR BERRIES.

LAZY SLOTH! HE'S LUCKY I DIDN'T EAT HIM!

I HAVE TO CLIMB ALL THAT WAY? YOU'VE GOT TO BE KIDDING ME!

OH WELL, HERE GOES NOTHING ...

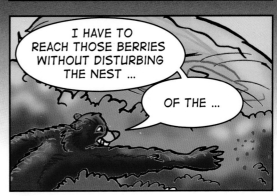

I HAVE TO REACH THOSE BERRIES WITHOUT DISTURBING THE NEST ...

OF THE ...

SCREEEECH!

GIANT VULTURE!

EARTH'S ICY PAST

TIME OUT!

For most of Earth's history, the climate has been much warmer than it is today. During these warm periods, there was no ice at the poles or even at the top of the tallest mountains.

However, there have been four major periods of cold weather in the planet's past. At these times, polar ice caps formed and large areas of the Earth were covered with thick sheets of ice. The earliest of these cold periods happened over 600 million years ago. The most recent cold period — the one we know as the Ice Age — began about two million years ago and ended about 11,000 years ago.

Scientists are uncertain about what causes an ice age to occur. The orbit of the Earth around the sun, the amount of carbon dioxide in the atmosphere, and the arrangement of continents are all factors that may combine to produce an ice age.

CHAPTER 2: The Glyptodont

URSULA BREAKS BRANCHES AS SHE FALLS.

WHOOSH!

THUD!

WH—WHAT HAPPENED?

SUCCESS ... BUT AT A PRICE — OUCH!

FOR YOUR SAKE, YOU'D BETTER HOPE THAT YOU'RE RIGHT.

AND YOU'D BETTER HOPE YOU DON'T RUN INTO THAT CAT THAT WAS AFTER HIM.

URSULA HEADS TOWARD THE SOUTHERN EDGE OF THE FOREST.

I LOST SOME VALUABLE TIME GOING FOR THOSE BERRIES!

I JUST CAN'T AFFORD ...

OH NO, A GLYPTODONT! FURTHER DELAYS!

MY NAME'S ROCA. WHO ARE YOU?

I'M URSULA. HAVE YOU SEEN MY BROTHER?

AS A MATTER OF FACT ... I THINK I HAVE.

WHERE? PLEASE TELL ME!

NOT SO FAST, SHORT-FACE ...

I NEED TO CROSS THE RIVER, AND YOU'RE GONNA TELL ME IF THE ICE IS THICK ENOUGH TO WALK ON.

THEN I'LL TELL YOU WHAT I KNOW ABOUT YOUR BROTHER!

YOU HAVE SOME NERVE, SHORT-FACE! IF YOU THINK I'M GOING TO HELP YOU NOW, THERE'S NO WAY!

TELL ME WHERE BRUNO WENT!

ROCA THE GLYPTODONT MOVES SLOWLY TO THE SIDE, AND SHOWS URSULA BRUNO'S FOOTPRINTS ON THE GROUND.

OK, OK ...

AS YOU CAN SEE, HE WENT THAT WAY!

ICE AGE

ANIMAL FACT FILE

Giant Ground Sloth

- One of the strangest mammals of the Ice Age
- Measured up to 20 ft. in length
- Weighed up to 6,000 lb.
- Huge claws were up to 20 in. long
- First lived in South America
- A herbivore — ate plants

Glyptodont (Glip-toh-dont)

- Distant relative of the armadillo
- Name means "carved tooth"
- Measured 5 ft. high and 10 ft. long
- Weighed as much as 2,000 lb.
- Covered in protective armor up to 2 in. thick
- Fossils found in Florida
- A slow-moving herbivore

Smilodon (Smy-loh-don)

- Closely related to modern cats, usually called "saber-toothed cat"
- Name means "knife-tooth"
- Measured 4 ft. at shoulder (compare lions at 3.5 ft.)
- Weighed up to 450 lb.
- Fossils of over 2,000 smilodons found in La Brea, California
- A carnivore — hunted other animals

YOU'RE IN THE WRONG PLACE AT THE WRONG TIME, BEAR!

MAYBE ...

MAYBE NOT!

ATTACK! NOW!

MORE DIRE WOLVES COME OUT OF THE FOREST!

GROOOWL!

GRRRRRR

WOLF ATTACK!

GROOOWL!

SNAP!

GOODBYE, SHORT-FACE ...

GRRRRRR!

UH-OH!

CREATING A MAMMOTH?

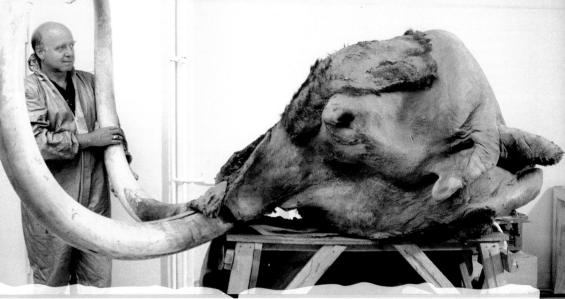

Bernard Buigues, a scientist who studies fossil animals and plants, is seen here with the head of the mammoth found in Siberia.

Have you ever wondered what it would be like to visit a real-life Jurassic Park? It may sound unbelievable, but you might be able to do this sooner than you think!

Right now, scientists are working on mapping and copying the genetic materials from a woolly mammoth. In December 2005, a group of researchers announced that they had already mapped one percent of a mammoth's genetic materials by using the remains of a 27,000-year-old mammoth found in Siberia.

The researchers think that if they can copy all of the mammoth's genetic materials, they might be able to create a new living mammoth. Other scientists are not so sure it can be done. They think that even if the researchers could copy the genetic materials, it would be too hard to create a living mammoth from them.

If the researchers succeed at creating a new mammoth, they might even be able to create a new dinosaur one day!

29

CHAPTER 4: The Caves of the Hunter

A CAVE!

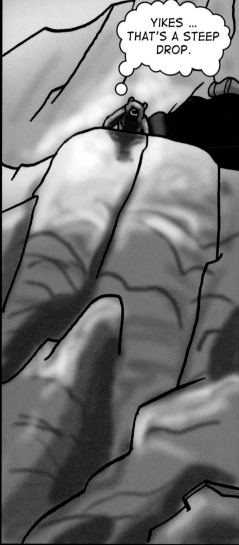

YIKES ... THAT'S A STEEP DROP.

I DON'T HAVE MUCH CHOICE, I GUESS.

URSULA WALKS SLOWLY THROUGH A DARK PASSAGE, WATCHING OUT FOR DANGER!

I'D BETTER BE CAREFUL ...

THE PEOPLE OF THE ICE AGE

TIME OUT!

During the Ice Age, much of the water on Earth turned into ice. Sea levels dropped to 330 ft. below present-day levels.

The narrow strip of sea separating Siberia and Alaska — the Bering Strait — was exposed as land. It was over this land bridge that humans are thought to have crossed from Asia into North America more than 13,000 years ago.

These people were the ancestors of the Native American peoples. They are called Paleo-Indians (ancient Indians). They made their tools and weapons out of stone. They were skilled hunters of large animals such as the woolly mammoth, bear, and bison.

The Paleo-Indians lived in caves and rock shelters. It is believed that they made beautiful paintings on rocks and cave walls. Many examples of rock art have been found in North America, but none have been proven to date from the end of the Ice Age.

Painting of a woolly mammoth

BACK IN THE CAVE WITH TUVAAQ.

AAH!

THE SPEAR FLIES PAST URSULA'S HEAD AND STICKS IN THE WALL!

WHY DID YOU DO THAT?

LOOK!

TRACKS!

TUVAAQ SAID I MUST GO SOUTH. SO SOUTH I MUST GO.

BEAR TRACKS!

AND SABERTOOTH TRACKS ... OH, NO!

IS BRUNO SAFE?

GOING, GOING, GONE

About 10,500 years ago, many unusual mammals in North America suddenly went extinct. Giant ground sloths, giant short-faced bears, saber-toothed cats, and glyptodonts were among the species that died out forever. What caused this?

One theory is that humans hunted these animals to extinction. In recent history, human hunting has caused the extinction of the dodo, the passenger pigeon, and the quagga (a close relative of the zebra).

Dodo

Passenger pigeon

Quagga

Some scientists believe climate change was a factor. Changes in the weather may have caused food sources to become scarce. This increased competition among different species for food.

Global Warming or Cooling?

Will we have another ice age? With all the recent talk about global warming, this might seem unlikely. But, think again …

Global temperatures increased by about 1 degree Fahrenheit in the 20th century. That may not sound like much, but many glaciers and ice sheets are melting fast. As polar ice melts and cold water is released into the North Atlantic, the warm ocean current known as the Gulf Stream may stop flowing. If this happens, parts of North America and Europe might be plunged into another ice age!

What causes global warming? When humans burn fossil fuels to fly planes, drive cars, and manufacture goods, a lot of gases and pollutants are released into the atmosphere. These gases and pollutants trap heat — like a greenhouse — and the result is global warming.

Scientists predict that temperatures will continue to rise in the 21st century, perhaps by as much as 10 degrees Fahrenheit. Whether this results in another ice age remains to be seen …

1979

2000

Dwindling Arctic ice
— notice the change
between 1979 and 2000

INDEX